DRESS CODE BLUES

Lenni pulled her notebook out of her book bag and began writing down her new song. Suddenly the words started jumping around on the page before her eyes. Ghostwriter!

The dancing letters came to a stop. Ghostwriter had scrambled them into a new message. It said: "DRESS CODE? IS THAT SOME KIND OF SECRET ALPHA-BET?"

Lenni shook her head. There were a lot of things about modern-day life that Ghostwriter had no clue about. She wrote her message back so Ghostwriter could understand it. Then she wrote a few quick sentences telling Ghostwriter about Ms. Willow and the dress code.

"WHAT ARE YOU GOING TO DO?" Ghostwriter asked.

"I DON'T KNOW," Lenni wrote back. "ANY IDEAS?"

"THINK ABOUT WHAT IS RIGHT," Ghostwriter wrote, "THEN DO IT."

Join the Team!

Do you watch GHOSTWRITER on PBS? Then you know that when you read and write to solve a mystery or unravel a puzzle, you're using the same smarts and skills the Ghostwriter team uses.

We hope you'll join the team and read along to help solve the mysterious and puzzling goings-on in these GHOSTWRITER books!

DRESS CODE MESS

BY

SARA ST. ANTOINE
ILLUSTRATED BY DAVE HENDERSON

A
CHILDREN'S TELEVISION WORKSHOP BOOK

BANTAM BOOKS
NEW YORK • TORONTO • LONDON • SYDNEY • AUCKLAND

DRESS CODE MESS

A Bantam Book / November 1992

Ghostwriter, **Ghost**writer *and* $\hat{\bullet}$ *are*
trademarks of Children's Television Workshop
All rights reserved. Used under authorization

Art direction by Marva Martin
Cover design by Susan Herr
Interior illustrations by Dave Henderson

ISBN 0-553-48071-5

Published simultaneously in the United States and Canada

Bantam Books are published by Bantam Books, a division of Bantam
Doubleday Dell Publishing Group, Inc. Its trademark, consisting of the
words "Bantam Books" and the portrayal of a rooster, is Registered
in U.S. Patent and Trademark Office and in other countries. Marca
Registrada. Bantam Books, 666 Fifth Avenue, New York, New York
10103.

PRINTED IN THE UNITED STATES OF AMERICA

OPM 0 9 8 7 6 5 4 3 2 1

DRESS CODE MESS

Lenni Frazier usually didn't mind listening to the principal's announcements. They came over the P.A. system every day at 2:50—right at the end of math class, just when she was too tired to think anymore.

But on this particular day there was a new voice on the P.A. system.

"Good afternoon, Zora Neale Hurston Middle School," the voice said. "My name is Ms. Henrietta Willow. I'm happy to announce that I'll be your acting principal for the rest of the term. I hope it will be a special time for all of us. I have lots of plans."

If Ms. Willow had suggested a fast-food counter in the lunchroom, she could have made herself the most popular acting principal in Hurston history. But instead she declared, "My first plan is to start a schoolwide dress code."

Dress code? What's that? wondered Lenni.

"I want all of you looking neater," Ms. Willow's voice explained. "It makes the school look bad when you come dressed in sloppy clothes. It's also distracting for you, the students, to have to spend so much time worrying about how you look. Studies have shown that students get better grades when they have a dress code. Tomorrow I want all of you to wear simple, neat clothes: pants—or skirts for the girls—and sweaters or plain shirts with collars. I'm sure you'll find it takes much less time to get dressed in the morning. And I'm sure we'll all find that it makes Hurston a better place for everyone. The dress code will be posted by my office in the morning. Thank you and have a good afternoon."

Lenni looked down at what she was wearing: leggings, an old, long sweatshirt, and red high tops. She was a dress code failure.

"This is ridiculous!" Lenni muttered. As soon as class ended, she grabbed her jacket from her locker. As she left the school, she passed Ms. Willow talking to the shop teacher. Ms. Willow looked at Lenni. Then she whispered out of the corner of her mouth to the other teacher, "This is the kind of thing I'm trying to change."

Lenni's face burned with anger—and humiliation. She needed to talk to her friends, Jamal Jenkins and Alex Fernandez.

Lenni, Jamal, and Alex were all members of the Ghostwriter team. Earlier in the year a ghost had started sending secret written messages to Jamal. Soon Lenni and Alex began to get messages, too. So did Alex's little sister, Gaby. It was hard to believe, but it was exciting at the same time. The kids promised each other not to tell anyone else about their secret friend unless Ghostwriter decided a new person was okay.

All they knew so far about Ghostwriter was that he had lived in the past and could communicate with them only through written or printed words. And that was also the only way the team could communicate back.

Together the Ghostwriter team had solved a lot of mysteries. They had also helped each other with some pretty tough problems. Now Lenni was hoping they'd have some ideas about how to deal with the dress code. When she found Alex and Jamal, they were playing one-on-one on the basketball courts behind the school.

"Can you believe it—a dress code?" she asked.

Jamal looked up, grinned, and passed the ball to Lenni. Without losing a beat, she caught it and dribbled the ball nearer the basket. Alex tried to check her, but Lenni swiveled away. She ducked past Alex, turned, jumped, and scored.

"Good move, Lenni," Jamal said enviously. "Why can't I be as fast as you—and as good a shot?"

The three friends played a friendly game for a while. Lenni put everything into it. She was smiling with her friends, but underneath she was still angry at that Ms. Willow. Before long, Alex's sister, Gaby, and her friend Tina Nguyen showed up. Tina was carrying a video camera.

"Hi, you guys," Gaby greeted them. "Anything worth taping here?"

Gaby planned to be a reporter. She loved to be in front of a video camera, and Tina loved to operate it, so together they made quite a team.

"We're getting scenes of life at middle school," Gaby explained. "According to the school bulletin, there are 425 kids in our elementary school. According to me and Tina, none of them has any idea what it will be like to go to middle school someday. So we're going to show them.''

"Gaby, let's tape these guys playing basketball. They're good!" Tina said.

"Don't tape us now," Alex shot back. "We're too tired. If you want to see *real* basketball, you should tape our pick-up game against the kids from Atlantic Avenue.''

"Think you're going to win?" Gaby asked hopefully.

Jamal shrugged and Alex gave him a friendly poke. "Bad question, right, Jamal?" he joked.

"Who's playing?" Tina asked.

"We've put together a pretty good team. Jamal's signed on Althea Gibb from the eighth grade. She's tall and fast. Then there's Cameron Wing, Judd Parsons, me—and our secret weapon," Alex boasted.

"We lost last year, but just barely." Jamal added. "The year before we lost by a lot. But this year we have the Lenni Machine.''

"Huh?" asked Gaby and Tina.

"Lenni is great! She's not tall, but she's fast, and she can jump. She can almost slam-dunk the ball!"

"Not really . . ." Lenni said modestly.

"Well, okay, maybe not by a long shot . . ." Jamal admitted. "But that's what I told those kids from Atlantic Avenue. I figured it wouldn't hurt to put a little scare into them.''

"Maybe we'll be lucky and win this time," Alex said optimistically.

"Hey, if the game is settled, can we talk about the dress code now?" Lenni asked, feeling a little frustrated.

"What dress code?" Tina asked.

4

"Our acting principal just told us she's starting a dress code at Hurston," Lenni explained. "Can you believe it?"

"Yuck," Gaby said, rolling her eyes. "What a pain!"

"Chill, you guys," Jamal said. "There's no reason to get upset about it—yet. We don't know what it means."

"What do you mean?" Gaby asked.

Jamal shrugged. "Maybe the rules will be easy to follow. Sometimes trying to keep up with everybody else is tough. King school just put in a dress code that says kids can't wear leather jackets to school. They're too expensive."

"Yeah. A friend of mine was beaten up and his jacket was stolen a couple of months ago," put in Alex. "There just might be some okay reasons for a dress code. It all depends."

"Don't you think we should do something now? No matter how simple it is, a dress code means you just can't be yourself," Lenni said.

"Maybe you should wait a few days and see what happens," Tina suggested.

"Trust me," Lenni said. "I already know it's going to be awful. I'm heading home. See you guys later."

It was good to get out on the street and have some space to think. The incident with Ms. Willow was really bugging Lenni. She kicked a can as she walked down the sidewalk in her neighborhood. As usual, there was a fat old bulldog sitting beside the newspaper stand on the corner. His tongue was sticking out, so Lenni stuck out her tongue back at him and kept walking. Then she laughed at herself.

As she walked along Oxford Avenue, she saw a guy sitting on a milk crate, playing his guitar and singing. He had long hair and was wearing jeans and sandals. Lenni stopped and listened to him for a while. He looked a lot like her father had looked in the seventies. Lenni kept a photo on her bulletin board of her dad and mom when they first met. The connection made Lenni realize that she needed to talk to her dad, so she hurried home.

Unfortunately, Max Frazier wasn't there. He'd left Lenni a note saying that he had an extra practice with his jazz band that afternoon and wouldn't be home until almost eight.

"Have a bowl of soup so you don't get too hungry," Max wrote in the note. "I'll pick up some Chinese food on the way home."

Lenni usually didn't mind being alone at home for the afternoon; in fact, she kind of liked it. Her mom had died when she was seven, so Lenni was used to taking care of herself. But today she really wanted to talk to her dad.

"Let's see, what kind of soup do we have?" she asked out loud as she opened up the cabinet. It was a choice between clam chowder and alphabet noodle. Lenni couldn't face the clam chowder, so she emptied the can of alphabet soup into a pot and put it on the stove. While she waited for it to heat up, she began hitting the counter with her wooden spoon. *Thump thump thump thump*. Then she added a can opener. *Thump tap thump tap thump tap thump!*

It was a good beat. "Alphabet, alphabet, alphabet soup! Alphabet, alphabet, alphabet soup!" Lenni said to the beat. Lenni took after her dad—she loved writing songs. She stirred the soup and brought up a spoonful of noodles. There was a *D*, a *P*, a *C*, and another *D*. Lenni began making up a song to go with the letters.

"*D* for Dress code—drives me mad.
P for Principal—she's bad.
C for Clothes—kids should choose.
D . . . *D* . . . what was *D* for?
D for Drive-me-crazy dress-code blues!"

While she sang, Lenni hit the counter and the pots with her makeshift drumsticks. Then she stirred the soup and came up with four new letters. This time she got a *U*, a *G*, and two *X*'s. Too hard. She stirred them in again and scooped up two more.

"*M* for Ms. Willow seems so mean.
S for She doesn't get the Hurston scene."

Thump tap thump tap thump tap thump! By now Lenni had pulled out a spatula, two forks, and a garlic press to help her with her percussion.

The soup was finally hot. Lenni poured some into a bowl and sat down at the kitchen table. She pulled her notebook out of her backpack and began writing down her new song.

Suddenly the words started jumping around on the page before her eyes. Ghostwriter!

Then the dancing letters came to a stop. Ghostwriter had scrambled them into a new message. It said: "DRESS CODE? IS THAT SOME KIND OF SECRET ALPHABET?"

Lenni shook her head. There were a lot of things about modern-day life that Ghostwriter had no clue about. She wrote her message back so Ghostwriter could understand

it. "IT'S A LIST OF THE KINDS OF CLOTHES YOU CAN AND CAN'T WEAR TO SCHOOL," she explained.

"YOU HAVE THAT MANY CLOTHES?" Ghostwriter wrote.

"Sure!" Lenni said with a laugh. Then she wrote a few quick sentences telling Ghostwriter about Ms. Willow and the dress code.

"WHAT ARE YOU GOING TO DO?" Ghostwriter asked.

"I DON'T KNOW," Lenni wrote back. "ANY IDEAS?"

"THINK ABOUT WHAT IS RIGHT," Ghostwriter wrote, "THEN DO IT."

Lenni rested her chin in her hand and thought awhile. She thought about the guy singing songs in the street, and then about her mom and dad. When they were young, they had stood up for what they believed in. Lenni thought some more about the dress code. She had to stand up for what *she* believed in, too. She felt almost as if she owed it to the memory of her mom. Then something caught her attention. Ghostwriter was sending her a message using the alphabet in her soup!

"ONE MORE VERSE?" he spelled out in the middle of her bowl.

Lenni laughed and stirred up the soup again.

> "*D* for Do what I feel's right.
> *P* for Protest; *F* for Fight."

Lenni paused. Her parents must have known exactly what they were doing. She wasn't quite as sure about herself. She stared at the letters in the bowl, then wrote her last line.

"*A* for Action; *N* for Now!"

That night Lenni told her dad about the dress code. He agreed that it sounded bad. "It limits your freedom," he told Lenni. "If you want, I'll go talk to the principal, this Ms. Willow."

But Lenni had her own ideas. She promised her dad she'd take care of it herself. Then after dinner she worked out her plan. "This will make Ms. Willow see that a dress code won't work at Hurston," she said to herself.

GET THE BEAT!

Lenni began her alphabet rap by banging on the counter with a spoon. She was setting the rhythm for her song. Rhythm is a song's inner drumbeat. It helps hold the song together.

Read the first two lines of Lenni's song:

> *D* for Dress code—drives me mad.
> *P* for Principal—she's bad.

There are seven beats in each line. If you go back and read the rest of Lenni's song, you'll see that once she set that seven-beat pattern, she followed it.

Here's a challenge. Pick a few letters from the alphabet. Using Lenni's seven-beat rhythm, write just one more verse for her poem!

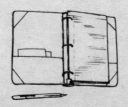

The next morning Lenni rummaged through the closet in her dad's room and pulled out two boxes of her mom's old clothes. She found short dresses, tie-dyed shirts, bell-bottom blue jeans, and a whole pile of bandannas. Finally she decided to wear an embroidered cotton blouse with a wide, floppy collar, a flowered skirt that came down to her ankles, a pair of her own lace-up boots, and several strands of beads.

Max was eating breakfast when Lenni came out. "Wow!" he said, putting down his coffee mug. "You do take after your mother! Peace!"

Lenni grinned and grabbed a bagel from the counter. "I'm protesting," she explained. "I know Ms. Willow is going to say this doesn't fit the code. Then I'm going to explain how it does fit—even though it's not her style. She'll see how tough it's going to be to set a dress code at Hurston. What do you think?"

"Almost perfect," Max said. "You just need one more thing. Hang on!" He got up from his chair and ran out of the room. When he came back a few minutes later, he had two buttons in his hand. One said Give Peace a Chance and another said Save the Whales.

"Thanks, Dad," Lenni said as she put the buttons on her shirt.

"Hey, Lenni?" Max said softly.

"Yeah?"

"You really remind me of your mom."

Lenni smiled and then headed confidently off to school. She found Jamal and Alex playing basketball on the playground.

"Yo, Lenni!" Jamal said with a grin when he saw her. "What's this—Halloween?"

"Protest clothes," Lenni offered. "Against the dress code."

"I thought we were going to talk to Ms. Willow before we did anything drastic," Jamal said.

Lenni shook her head. "We can't wait. We have to act now. Before she can make it stick."

"You sound like one of those guys handing out pamphlets in the subway," Jamal said.

"Come on, you two. Enough talking," Alex said. "We've got a basketball game next week, and we've gotta start practicing. And by the way, Lenni, how are you going to play in that outfit?"

"Easy!" Lenni tucked her long skirt up at the waist. Now her Georgetown gym shorts peeked out from under the hem of the skirt.

"Let's smear Alex," Jamal said with a friendly grin as he passed the ball.

Lenni dribbled across the court and took a shot at the

basket. It didn't even bounce off the backboard; it went right in.

Alex grabbed the ball and went out to get his shot. But as he dribbled, Lenni got the ball. She pivoted. She dodged Alex. She passed to Jamal. Alex tried to check Jamal's shot. Jamal passed back to her. She jumped. She shot another basket! Yes!!! Lenni was beginning to think this was *her* day.

"All right!" Jamal said, running up and giving her a high-five.

"Yeah, well, I wasn't covering her," Alex said, taking the ball.

"No excuses, Alex," Jamal laughed. "Practice again this afternoon?" he suggested.

"I can't," Alex said. "I have to work at the bodega." His parents owned a small grocery store, and he and Gaby sometimes helped out there after school.

"I'll practice, Jamal," Lenni said. "Meet you here at three o'clock sharp."

Lenni headed into the building, amazed to see that just about all the kids were trying to dress according to Ms. Willow's rules. "They just don't appreciate a good protest," she decided when some of them teased her about her clothes.

But by the end of the day she still hadn't seen Ms. Willow. Her protest spirit had begun to fade. She put the dress code out of her head and hurried to her locker so she wouldn't be late to meet Jamal. She didn't notice the tall woman in blue following her down the hall. The woman was writing on a clipboard. As Lenni was putting her books away, she noticed a sign on the wall. It usually said KNOW YOUR LOCKER COMBINATION! Now Ghostwriter was scrambling some of the letters. LOOK OUT! the sign said—and no wonder . . .

Lenni turned around to see the woman in the blue suit peering down at her and writing her name on the clipboard.

"Yes, ma'am?" Lenni asked.

"Did you hear my announcement yesterday about the dress code?" It was Ms. Willow!

Lenni swallowed hard and nodded. Something about Ms. Willow made her want to disappear into her locker.

"Then why are you dressed as you are?"

Lenni stood up a little straighter. "What's wrong with my outfit? It's a skirt that *I* think is neat, and a shirt with a collar. Sounds like it meets the dress code, even if you don't like it." She tried hard to make that last part sound respectful.

She continued, "I think we should get to wear whatever we feel like wearing. It's more creative."

"So is painting the school pink and purple, but that doesn't make it right, does it?"

"Well, it also limits our freedom," Lenni said, remembering what her father had said the night before.

"Going to school at all limits your freedom, doesn't it, Lenni?" Ms. Willow asked.

Lenni couldn't think of what to say next. Was this how protests were supposed to go?

Ms. Willow shook her head. "Young lady," she said, "you look like something right out of the 1960s."

"Hey, these were my mom's," Lenni said defensively. She was thinking about what her father had said to her that morning . . . how her mother would have been proud of her. Ms. Willow had no right to put her down.

"Well, your mother ought to know that these clothes are not right for school in the 1990s," Ms. Willow said.

She doesn't know what she's saying, Lenni thought angrily. But she didn't say anything back. Instead, she waited while Ms. Willow took down her name and gave her a warning. Four warnings and she'd have to serve a detention—stay after school.

"Dear," Ms. Willow said finally, "just think how much easier it will be if you just wear something normal." She smiled and continued down the hall.

Lenni slammed the door to her locker. What had gone wrong? So much for my one-woman protest, Lenni thought. She headed outside to find Jamal.

He was sitting on a basketball at the edge of the playground. "You're too late," he said, pointing at the group of boys playing on the court. "These guys took over a few minutes ago."

"Sorry," Lenni said.

"I thought you said you'd be here at three o'clock sharp," Jamal said, standing up and walking with her away from the court.

"I got kind of stuck."

"Doing what?" Jamal asked.

Lenni hesitated. Then she blurted out, "Ms. Willow said I was disobeying the dress code. Made me mad. But I'll handle it," she said. Then she cheered up. "Hey, want to go play video games?"

Jamal shook his head. "I have a test tomorrow."

"Well, I'll see ya later then."

"Sure," Jamal said. "And let's make sure you don't get stuck again. Maybe if we both went to talk to Ms. Willow, she would understand how we feel. I tell you what. Let's dress very carefully tomorrow, so we don't get in trouble with her. And we'll talk to her before school starts." He gave Lenni a friendly punch in the arm and took off down the street.

When Lenni turned the corner, she came across Tina and Gaby carrying all their video equipment.

"Oh no, we're too late," Gaby wailed when she saw Lenni.

"For what?" Lenni asked.

"We wanted to get some footage of kids around school," Tina explained. "But I guess no one will be around now."

"Oh, you'll be able to find some people," Lenni assured them. "Especially the ones involved in sports or clubs. And those are the really important things to film anyway."

"Oh good!" Gaby said, cheering up. "Hey, Lenni," she added, eyeing Lenni's outfit. "Wild clothes."

Lenni rolled her eyes and ignored the comment. "You ought to see lots of teachers hanging around the school, too," she said with a scowl as she thought about Ms. Willow. Tina seemed to like the idea.

"It'll be great to interview them, too," she said. "Ele-

mentary kids need to know that middle-school teachers aren't monsters."

"But they are!" Lenni exclaimed. She almost smiled as she pictured Ms. Willow growing horns and fangs.

"They are?" Gaby asked, looking a little reluctant to head toward the school now.

"She's just kidding," Tina said. She grabbed Gaby by the arm and started pulling her away. "See ya, Lenni!"

Lenni waved good-bye and decided to head over to the park. She usually sat on a bench under a tree. From there she could see all the action: high school kids hanging out around a central fountain, skateboarders and rollerbladers zipping by, mothers pushing babies in their strollers, old ladies throwing crumbs to the pigeons.

As she sat down on the bench, Lenni decided it might help Tina and Gaby out if she wrote a song to go with their video. She already had a title: "Where the Teachers Are Monsters."

Lenni started by thinking of all sorts of things that had scared her about middle school before she got there. She remembered thinking the big kids would push her around. She'd been sure she'd forget the combination to her locker. And she'd been terrified of getting lost in the halls. Lenni wrote these ideas and others in a list in her notebook. Then she started her song.

> Your teachers
> Are monsters;
> They haven't got a heart . . .

Lenni stopped to think of something that rhymed with heart. Cart. Dart. Chart. Start. That was it!

> They'll kill you with homework.
> They're tough right from the start!

Lenni looked down at her list and started in on the next line.

> The hallways
> Are mazes.
> You're lost without a map.

Lenni wanted to make that part even more dramatic. First she had to find a word that rhymed with map. Tap. Nap. Flap. Trap. Yes, trap!

> Just ask the kid who missed a turn
> And fell into a trap!

Lenni smiled. What next? She looked out at the people in the park and saw a jogger go by with a whistle around his neck. That gave her an idea.

> The coaches
> Use approaches
> That run you to the ground.

This time when Lenni looked out, she noticed a lady selling hot dogs from a food cart and got an idea for her next verse.

>   The lunch food
>   Is awful.
>   It's from the lost and found.

Lenni realized this could go on forever. Let's see, what would be a good way to wind it up?

>   The big kids
>   Are bullies
>   They pick on kids your size.
>   So, BE SMART!
>   And BEWARE!
>   Even I've been spinning a few lies
>   Just to give you kids a scare.

Lenni read over her song again and laughed. Maybe this wasn't exactly what Gaby and Tina would want, but she had fun writing it. And the best thing was that it had almost made her forget her problems with Ms. Willow.

MAKE A LIST

Imagine this: Your teacher asks you to write a poem. You draw a blank. You can't get any good ideas. What should you do?

First, think about what you want to write about—your main idea. Then, on a separate piece of paper, jot down every idea that comes to mind when you say that idea to yourself. You don't have to write complete sentences. Ideas, names, words—even scribbles and doodles will help. When you can't come up with any new thoughts, you have your list.

Take the words and phrases and ideas from your list. Use them to write a poem or paragraph. You can even write your poem in the form of a list:

> Ms. Willow
> Seems hard-hearted,
> Up-front, tough,
> Has her own ideas,
> Gives you a hard
>   time—
> But what's she really
>   like?

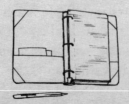

T he next day Lenni put on a plain shirt and a short denim skirt. It took her a while to find something in her closet that she thought Ms. Willow might approve of. Jamal was probably right, though, she thought. They shouldn't get Ms. Willow upset about their clothes while they were trying to get her to listen about the dress code.

When she met Jamal at school, he was wearing clean denim pants and a mock turtleneck shirt. They spotted Ms. Willow right away. She was standing outside the office.

Before Jamal could say a word, she looked at Lenni and said, "Your skirt is too short." Then she turned to Jamal and said, "And you are violating the code, too. It says shirts with collars. A turtleneck doesn't count."

She jotted down their names on a clipboard that seemed to have a million names on it. Then she turned on her heel and went back to her office to answer the phone.

"I can't believe this!" Jamal said through gritted teeth. "She never gave us a chance!" He reached down to pick up a workbook sheet that had fallen out of his notebook. As he glanced at it, the words rearranged themselves. Ghostwriter! "Look at this, Lenni!"

The words now said, "LOTS OF NAMES ON THE

VIOLATION LIST. LENNI FRAZIER, JAMAL JENKINS, ALFONSO RAMIREZ, LEE KIANG . . ." The list went on.

"That's practically the whole seventh grade," Jamal pointed out.

"Everybody but Calvin Ferguson," Lenni said. "He just fits the dress code perfectly. And I bet he loves watching everybody else get warnings!" (Calvin was not one of Lenni's favorite people.)

By the end of the school day kids were getting warnings like crazy. Some teachers were trying to make kids stick to it. Others didn't try. But it seemed like nobody really understood the code. Ms. Willow kept posting copies, but some prankster kept tearing them off the bulletin board. Jamal was sure *that* was Calvin.

That afternoon Lenni told her dad that she might want to transfer to another school. "I'd like to try a school for the performing arts," she told him.

"Is it so bad at Hurston now?" Max asked. "I thought you liked it there."

Lenni didn't feel like explaining. Her dad had been so proud of her for being a rebel. She didn't want to disappoint him. "Can I play your keyboard for a while?" she asked, changing the subject.

"Sure," her dad said. "But wear the headphones, would you? And tell me what's going on at school."

"Oh, Ms. Willow hates me, that's all," Lenni said with a sigh. Lenni gave in and told her dad about the warnings she'd earned.

"That's ridiculous!" he snapped. "I saw you today. You

were dressed perfectly decently. How could anyone give you a warning for that?" He continued, "If Hurston needs a dress code, okay—but it better be clear and it better be fair. I think I'll pay this Ms. Willow a visit tomorrow."

"Dad, I don't want you to get too upset," Lenni protested. "I can handle this. Jamal is already with me. Lots of other kids have begun getting in trouble with the code, too. I think Ms. Willow just doesn't realize what she's doing. We're trying to find a way to make her understand." Lenni gave her dad her most confident smile, then beat a retreat to the other room. Soon she was banging away on his keyboard. She was trying to come up with a song that would make her feel better.

> "When you're feeling not so happy, but you want
>   to stand up tall;
> You've got to shake off all your troubles, hold
>   your head high, show 'em all. . . ."

After a minute she laughed. Boy, am I taking myself seriously, she thought. So she added,

> "Why not put on funky colors, dye your shoes
>   or dye your hair . . ."

What did she want to say now? She said the line over a few times, and still she was drawing a blank. Should she add more things to the list? Should she change the mood?

"Okay," Lenni said out loud. "Let's see . . . 'Put on lots of funky colors, dye your shoes or dye your hair . . .'"

"And if you're really feeling crazy, you can dye your underwear!" a voice shouted.

Lenni spun around and took off her headphones. Jamal was sitting on a chair behind her with a big grin on his face. "Jamal! You scared me! What are you doing here?"

"I thought we ought to plan our strategy with Ms. Willow better this time. Your dad let me in, and I've been sitting here for five minutes waiting for you to notice me. What are you writing?" he asked.

"It's a song about feeling okay about yourself. Sort of. I'm going to switch to another section now."

"Go ahead," Jamal said. "I'll just sit here quietly and do my math homework till you're done."

"You sure?" Lenni asked suspiciously. "You're not going to jump in with a dumb line again, are you?"

"No. Promise," Jamal said. When Lenni put her headphones on again, he added, ". . . that it won't be dumb."

Lenni found it easy to choose the next line. "If . . . you're . . . really feeling awful, you can dress for that mood, too."

Jamal jumped in quickly. "Just wear skirts down to your ankles like Lenni here would do!"

"Jamal!" Lenni said crossly, throwing down her headphones.

"What's wrong, Lenni?"

"You're spoiling my song!"

"No, I'm making it better."

"You just think you're smart because you can come up with rhymes so fast."

"Well, yes," Jamal said with a grin. He jumped up and

hit a few notes on the keyboard. "Let's see if you can! Try this: 'If you're feeling really sporty, here's the thing you ought to wear . . .'"

"Um . . . 'Big pads on both your shoulders and a helmet on your hair!'" Lenni said. That made Jamal crack up and then Lenni started laughing, too. "All right," she said. "What if you're feeling mean?"

"'You should paint your face bright green!'" Jamal said. "And if you're feeling obnoxious?"

Lenni rolled her eyes, then burst out laughing. "'Then dress like Ms. Willow!'" she said between giggles.

"That doesn't rhyme!" Jamal laughed.

"Oh, who cares," Lenni said. She was laughing so hard now, she could barely speak. "How about if you're feeling orange?"

"Orange?" Jamal asked, giving up. "Orange?" This time he was laughing just as hard as Lenni.

"Just kidding," Lenni said between snorts of laughter. "Everyone knows nothing rhymes with orange."

Just then there was a knock on the door. It was Alex, Gaby, and Tina.

"We thought you guys might be here," Alex said. "Come on, we need to practice for the big game!"

"And we need more footage," Gaby said. "We spent an hour taping the teachers after school. Now we need more kids."

"First we need to talk about the dress code," Jamal said. "Right, Lenni?"

She smiled, and together they filled the other kids in on their battles with Ms. Willow.

"Wow," Alex said, taking off his jacket and sitting down. "Ms. Willow has only been here two weeks and already she hates you."

"Alex!" Gaby said. "Don't tell Lenni that!" She turned to look at Lenni. "I think Ms. Willow's being totally unfair." She pointed her finger at Alex and added, "You should wear what Lenni wore and see what happens."

"I'm not wearing beads!" Alex protested.

"Lenni! That reminds me," said Jamal. "I found out today that you have a fan club at school. Some girls have decided to wear long skirts and big blouses like the stuff you wore. I guess they think there's no point in trying to live up to this dress code. They said they get warnings no matter what they wear, so they might as well have some fun."

"I think you guys are missing the point," Tina said, "which is that Ms. Willow hasn't been fair. I don't think the answer is to wear weird clothes to school . . ."

"Weird?!" Lenni exclaimed.

". . . or outrageous or torn or whatever," Tina went on. "You've been treated unfairly. You should complain."

"Oh, come on, I want to see Alex in beads!" Gaby said.

"I don't think you guys understand," Tina said.

"Understand what, Tina?" Lenni asked.

The other kids looked up expectantly. At first Tina just looked at her video camera and moved the power switch absentmindedly. "I don't know," she said in a quiet voice. "It's just that we're really lucky in this country to have a right to say what we think about something. A lot of people in other countries can't do that."

Something about the way Tina was talking made everyone hush up. "If we think the dress code is unfair to Lenni or anyone else, then we should make sure we put that in writing. And we should make sure we get a fair hearing."

"Why don't we all try to come up with some suggestions after practice? Then tomorrow we can put together a really awesome plan," Alex suggested.

Everyone agreed.

"Sounds good to me," Lenni said happily. Nothing seemed as bad now that she had four friends helping her out.

"Now it's time for action," Gaby said, jumping off her chair. "We need to tape Basketball Practice—Part One!"

As the kids headed out the door, Lenni gave Jamal a high-five. "Thanks, Jamal," she said.

"For coming up with such excellent rhymes for your song?" he asked with a grin.

"Yeah, that and other things," Lenni said. And they headed off to practice.

RHYME TIME

Sometimes it's easy to find words that rhyme—they just pop into your head. But here are some things to do if that doesn't work:

- Try replacing the first letter of the word you're trying to rhyme with different letters of the alphabet.
- If you're trying to find a rhyme for a long word, look at just the end of the word first.
- Finally, if you do something crazy like end a line with "orange," you might get stuck forever trying to find a rhyme. Maybe the best thing to do is to get rid of "orange"! Would "yellow" work just as well?

Now tackle some rhymes on your own. How many rhymes can you find for these words:

DRESS   CODE   LENNI   SCHOOL   WILLOW

After you find your rhymes, try turning some of the words into a poem. It's fine if it's a nonsense poem.

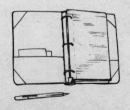

The next day Lenni found Alex at a table in the cafeteria.

"Where's Jamal?" she asked as she sat down with her tray.

"At a meeting," Alex said, moving his tray to give her more room. "Come up with any great ideas about the dress code?"

Lenni shook her head. "Not yet. You know, I'd like to see this dress code. It's hard to complain about it when we don't really know what it says."

"Well, somebody keeps swiping it every time Ms. Willow posts it. But maybe we could ask her for a copy."

"I'd rather serve detention," Lenni grumbled.

"Then I'll ask," Alex said.

"No, wait, I have a better idea. Let's see if Ghostwriter can find it," Lenni said. She pulled out her pen and wrote Ghostwriter a message. "CAN YOU FIND US A COPY OF THE DRESS CODE?"

Ghostwriter wrote back: "WHAT DOES A DRESS CODE LOOK LIKE?"

Lenni and Alex looked at each other and shrugged. Finally Alex wrote, "IT SHOULD BE SOME KIND OF LIST OF RULES. ALL ABOUT CLOTHES."

"I'LL TRY," Ghostwriter wrote back—and left.

Lenni and Alex finished their lunch. "Guess it'll take a while," Lenni said after they'd cleaned up and started heading out of the cafeteria. But just then Lenni noticed the milk carton one of her friends was about to throw away.

"Hey, Janet! Wait up!" Lenni yelled, lunging for the carton. She knocked it right out of her friend's hand, spilling chocolate milk all over the front of her own sweater.

"Lenni, what are you doing?" Janet asked.

"Sorry," Lenni said. "Ugh, what a mess." She grabbed a handful of napkins and tried to soak up some of the chocolate milk. Instead she ended up smearing it even more.

"Why'd you do that?" Alex asked as they walked away.

"Ghostwriter was sending us a message," Lenni said, holding up the milk carton. She was right. The letters on the side of the carton now said, "READ JAMAL'S COMPUTER TONIGHT."

"Tonight?! Ghostwriter had all day to tell me that," Lenni exclaimed. "Why did I risk my life trying to grab that milk carton?" She tried again to wipe off the chocolate stain. But it was no use.

"Well, I hope this means he found the dress code," Alex said.

"Me, too," Lenni said. "I'll see you at practice, okay?"

"Sure thing," Alex said, heading in the opposite direction.

Lenni looked down at her sweater. What if Ms. Willow

saw this? She'd never understand! And Lenni would have her third warning! "Uh oh," she said under her breath and began racing toward her classroom. She sprinted around the first corner so fast that she ran right into a person walking the other way. As luck would have it, that person was Ms. Willow.

"Hello, Lenni," she said.

"Hi, Ms. Willow," Lenni said meekly.

"That's a lovely sweater, Lenni," Ms. Willow said. "I'm sorry you didn't wash it before wearing it to school today."

"I did wash it, Ms. Willow. This just happened today at lunch!" Lenni explained. "See, it's still . . ."

"You're testing me, Lenni, aren't you? But it won't work. I'm tired of seeing you so ill-clad."

Ill-clad. Lenni repeated the word in her head. It definitely sounded like a disease.

"That makes three warnings, doesn't it? One more and I'll have to give you a detention next Monday afternoon for an hour and a half. I'd rather not. I'm having to give out an awful lot of warnings. I wish I could make you students understand that this dress code is to make your lives easier. Have a nice day," Ms. Willow said and headed off down the hall.

"Ugh," Lenni said.

"She's just plain rotten!" Alex complained later that afternoon when Lenni told him the bad news.

"She's the meanest lady I've ever known," Jamal agreed. "What will we do if you get detention? You'll miss the basketball game!"

Lenni shook her head. "I won't let her catch me at anything. I'll be careful."

The minute school was over, Jamal, Lenni, and Alex met the rest of their pick-up team to practice. It was a relief to be out of school and playing basketball. Jamal was having a really good day. Alex was handing off the ball, passing it between his legs, trying to jam the ball into the net. Lenni was all over the court. She darted around Althea. She wouldn't budge when Alex tried to rush her. Then she tripped as she was trying to avoid Jamal. *Thunk!!* She was on the ground. "I'll take a little time out," she panted, out of breath. She moved to the sidelines. She sat down beside Gaby and Tina, who were taping the practice.

While she was getting her breath back, Lenni started to notice the sounds of the game. The sneakers *skreeked* when the players pivoted on the court. The ball swished through the basket. It sounded something like *bwaank* when it bounced off the backboard. Two players bumped into each other and it sounded like *shlumpfff*.

Lenni took out her notebook and started writing down the odd sounds as she heard them.

At one point the words began to scramble up. It was Ghostwriter again. "WHAT'S GOING ON THERE?" he asked.

"THE KIDS ARE PLAYING BASKETBALL," Lenni wrote back.

"BASKETBALL?" Ghostwriter asked.

"IT'S A SPORT," Lenni wrote.

"MY GOODNESS!" Ghostwriter wrote back. "I FEEL LIKE I CAN PRACTICALLY HEAR IT!!"

He seemed awfully happy.

Lenni tried to think of more words.

"What are you doing, Lenni?" Tina asked, as she and Gaby came over to sit beside her.

"Trying to describe basketball in sounds alone," Lenni said. "Are you done with your videotaping? Do you want to help?"

They nodded, and Lenni explained the kinds of words she was looking for. Gaby came up with "splash," "zip," and "hoot." "That's us—hooting on the sidelines," she explained.

Tina suggested "slam" and "crash" and "swish." "You know, the sound a basketball makes going through the hoop."

When Lenni finished, Ghostwriter sent her a message. "THANKS FOR ALL THE NOISES," he wrote. "THIS BASKETBALL SPORT OF YOURS SEEMS A LOT MORE EXCITING NOW!"

Lenni smiled. Then she folded up her notebook and went back on the court.

"Do you really think you have what it takes to beat those guys on Monday?" Tina asked when they were through.

"Absolutely," Lenni said. "We can be great. I know it!"

SOUND OFF!

Lenni wrote to Ghostwriter using a special group of words. All of them sound like the action they describe. (Other words in this group are ones like "bang" and "fizz" and "snip.") They're all examples of *onomatopoeia* (pronounced on-a-ma-toe-pee-a). Luckily, you don't have to be able to pronounce onomatopoeia to use those kinds of words.

Make a list of noise words that exist—like "splash," "zip," "thrash," "buzz," "roar." How many noise words can you think of?

When you run out of noise words that exist, make up some of your own.

Pretend you are writing to Ghostwriter. Write a poem or paragraph that uses noise words. Try one of these topics or make up your own.

- Try describing a baseball game with sounds.
- Describe a puppy in a mud puddle on a rainy day.
- Pretend you got locked in a dark basement. What do you hear?

On Friday night Lenni, Alex, and Gaby gathered around Jamal and his computer. "Let's hope Ghostwriter got that dress code," Lenni said.

Moments later words began to appear on the screen. "DRESS REQUIREMENTS FOR GIRLS AND BOYS."

"That's it!" Alex exclaimed. "Good job, Ghostwriter!"

"Sure sounds stuffy," Gaby said.

"Look, there are the rules," Lenni said, as more words began to appear on the screen.

DRESS REQUIREMENTS FOR GIRLS AND BOYS

1. There will be no athletic shoes worn except in gym class.
2. Boys may not wear blue jeans.
3. Girls and boys must wear sweaters or plain cotton shirts with collars.
4. Girls' skirts should cover the knee.
5. Hair should be neat at all times.
6. Girls may not wear any jewelry.

"I don't get it!" Alex exclaimed. "How come only the boys can't wear blue jeans? And what about black jeans?"

"Don't complain," Lenni said. "It looks like only the girls can't wear jewelry."

"There's something else that isn't fair," Gaby said. "I know we videotaped teachers wearing shirts without collars. And some of them were even wearing jeans. Don't they have to obey the dress code, too?"

Jamal printed out a copy of the dress code and read it over one more time. "This is confusing," he said, shaking his head. "Ghostwriter was right."

As if on cue, Ghostwriter started scrambling the words in a message. "WHAT ABOUT ANKLES?"

"What does he mean by that?" Gaby asked, starting to giggle.

"He must be talking about item four, where it says that skirts should cover girls' knees," Lenni said. She wrote a quick note to Ghostwriter to make sure.

"EXACTLY," he wrote back. "YOU DON'T EXPOSE YOUR LIMBS, DO YOU?"

That made everyone laugh. "I wish Ghostwriter could see a picture of Madonna!" Gaby exclaimed.

"GHOSTWRITER," Lenni wrote, "PEOPLE WEAR SHORT SKIRTS ALL THE TIME."

"Wait a sec!" Jamal exclaimed. "Ghostwriter made me think of something. This dress code must be old. Really old."

"As old as Ghostwriter?" Gaby asked.

"Who knows? But that's why it says boys can't wear

blue jeans and doesn't say anything about girls. Because girls wouldn't even think of wearing blue jeans back then."

"Right!" Gaby said. "It could be from before the 1960s. I was reading a book about the history of dungarees last week. It was called *Blue Jeans*. It mentioned that girls always wore dresses to school until the 1960s. Then jeans became popular."

"We have to get the school to rewrite this dress code," said Jamal. "It's too confusing. And it's also not fair."

"Great idea," Gaby said immediately. "Let's write the school a letter. For starters, ask them whether or not it applies to teachers, too."

"Good. Write that down," Lenni instructed. "And while you're at it, write 'What's the big deal about collars?'"

"And make them see how stupid it is in the 1990s to say that only boys can't wear blue jeans," Alex said.

"And about those athletic shoes. Does that include high tops? Tennis shoes? Running shoes?" Jamal added. "Who wears anything else?"

"And what about this neat hair thing?" Gaby added. "Who decides what's neat and what isn't?"

The kids wrote all of their questions and comments very neatly beside each item on the dress code. Luckily there was lots of room on the paper. When they were through, they wrote a letter to their counselor, Mr. Brown.

"He'll be more understanding than Ms. Willow," Lenni insisted.

They stapled their questions to the letter and put everything in an envelope.

"Let's take this in Monday morning before school," Jamal suggested. "And Lenni, you be careful. Stay out of Ms. Willow's way."

Monday morning the kids met on the school playground before the bell rang. Alex, Lenni, and Jamal were nervous. First, they were worried about what their counselor would think of their letter. And mostly they were nervous about the game that afternoon.

"Come on, you guys, we've got to get to Mr. Brown soon, or he'll be busy with conferences," Alex said.

The three kids trooped inside and went down to the main office. The receptionist was there, but she told the kids Mr. Brown was out for the whole morning.

"He's making arrangements for tomorrow night's PTA meeting," she explained.

"Oh, bummer," Lenni sighed.

"We were hoping to give him a letter about the dress code," Alex explained. "Do you know when he'll get back?"

"Oh, the dress code? Why, I believe that's Ms. Willow's department," the receptionist said. "And look, here she is now. I'm sure she'll be happy to take a look at your letter."

The kids had no way to escape—just then Ms. Willow came in the door. "What's this? A letter for me?" she asked.

"Yeah," Jamal said, handing her the letter. The two others automatically started looking over their clothes. Especially Lenni. She had just realized, with horror, that a long sweatshirt over leggings wasn't going to count as a dress. She tried to melt into the background so Ms. Willow wouldn't notice her.

"Humph," Ms. Willow said as she took the letter from Jamal. She tucked it into the pocket of her jacket as if she wasn't even going to read it. "It's rather strange that the three of you should be bringing up the dress code," she said, turning her eyes on the kids. "You're certainly not following it, are you?"

"Uh oh," Alex said under his breath.

"I'm afraid I have to give all of you a warning," she said. Then she turned her attention to Lenni. "Don't even try to hide that sweatshirt," she said. "You're up to four warnings, aren't you, Lenni? I believe that means you have a detention study hall this afternoon. Give your names to Ms. Clementi."

"Man, Lenni, this is rough," Jamal said.

"Yeah, there goes the game," said Alex.

"Ah, come on, guys," Lenni pleaded. "You know you can win without me!" She felt awful about the detention. She really had tried to avoid it. Just then the morning bell rang, and she gestured down the hall. "I think I'll go," she said.

"Poor Lenni," Jamal said, shaking his head as they watched her go down the hall. "There's gotta be something more we can do."

"We should at least go talk to her before the game," Alex said.

He met Lenni at her locker right after school. She was packing up her backpack.

"Where are you going?" he asked her.

"To play basketball," she said with determination. "I can't sit in one place for another hour or I'll go crazy."

"You're really going to play?" Alex asked.

"Sure," she said. "I'll do triple detentions next week, maybe. But this game is important!"

Just then they heard a loud whoop, and saw Jamal sprinting toward them at full speed.

"What's up with him?" Lenni asked.

As soon as Jamal reached them, he started spilling out his story. "I was in history class this afternoon," he said. "We've been studying our government—especially the Bill of Rights." He caught his breath. "The point is, the Bill of Rights says we all have a right to free speech."

"If we had to pay for it, I'd be in trouble," Lenni joked.

"You know what I mean, Lenni. 'Free' meaning nobody can stop you or hold you back. You're free to say whatever you believe . . . like Tina was talking about last week. Anyway, Mr. Kent, our history teacher, said free speech means we have the right to complain about things we think are unfair—as loud as we want to."

Lenni leaned her head back. "I hate the dress code!!" she screamed at the top of her lungs.

Alex and Jamal laughed and Lenni smiled—that felt good. But Jamal told them something that made her feel even better.

"I talked to Mr. Kent about the dress code after class," Jamal said. "And you know what? I think he hates it, too. He said he'd rather spend his time teaching than giving kids warnings about wearing T-shirts. He thought our letter was a good idea and said we should try again to get it to Mr. Brown. Then he came up with an awesome idea. He thought maybe we could speak at the PTA meeting tomorrow night."

"Us?!" Lenni exclaimed. "They'll never let us!"

"Yes, they will," Jamal said with a huge smile. "Never underestimate the powers of a history teacher."

Jamal said they'd been given five minutes to present their dress code concerns to the PTA. He said he thought Lenni should give the speech, since she'd been the one most affected by the dress code.

"Me? I can't write speeches," Lenni said.

"Sure you can," Alex said. "You're always writing stuff."

"Raps. Songs. Not speeches!" Lenni argued.

"Then write a rap," Jamal said.

"Right," Lenni said. "That would really thrill the parents."

"I think it's a great idea!" Alex said.

"Why wouldn't they let you do a rap?" Jamal asked. "Come on, you should be able to explain yourself any way you want. Isn't that sort of what free speech is all about?"

He had a point. Lenni finally agreed and said she'd start in on the rap right after the game.

"Are you sure you want to play in the game today?" Alex asked. "I mean, what's the point of getting in more trouble?"

"I think he's right," Jamal said.

"Go write, Lenni," Alex advised her. "We'll be okay. You need all the time you can get to write that rap."

"You're sure?" Lenni asked.

Just then Tina and Gaby came down the hall. "I thought we were going to meet out front," Gaby said. "Come on, we'll be late for the game!"

Alex filled Gaby and Tina in on Lenni's detention—and her chance to be a rap star at the PTA meeting. "In that case," Tina said, "we should quickly give Lenni some ideas about what to put in her rap."

Lenni got out a pencil and a notebook and began to jot down their suggestions. They all agreed she should talk about the old dress code and why it was outdated. Alex thought she should ask the audience to look at what they were wearing and see if they'd pass the dress code requirements. Tina thought Lenni should explain how unfairly she'd been treated. Jamal thought she should point out that jeans were an important part of everyone's wardrobe. Gaby had so many ideas, Lenni could barely write them all down.

"Explain that you have to be in fashion or people will call you a geek. Explain that you can't run fast in long skirts and ask how long the collars have to be and find out why they didn't ask about socks. Tell them the kids in elementary school don't have dress codes and they probably would be afraid to come here if they knew. Tell them about the teachers who didn't pass the dress code in our video and tell them . . ."

"Enough, Gaby!" Alex said, pushing her toward the door. Lenni wrote the last ideas down, wished Alex and Jamal good luck with the game, and watched them head off down the hall. Then she headed into study hall. "Once again, on my own," she said under her breath. She was beginning to get tired of it.

Lenni sat down at an empty table and began looking over her notes. It was hard to concentrate, and she found herself staring out the window. She wanted to be out on the basketball court with her friends.

She looked down at her notes again, but this time there was a message from Ghostwriter on the page. "GREETINGS, LENNI," he wrote. "HOW'S LIFE?"

"BAD," Lenni wrote back.

"BAD?" Ghostwriter wrote. "WHAT DO YOU MEAN BY THAT?"

"LONELY," Lenni wrote this time.

"OH."

Lenni told Ghostwriter why she was stuck in study hall and how she was supposed to be writing the dress code speech. "IT IS EXCITING," she wrote. "BUT I MISS PLAYING WITH THE TEAM."

"YOU MAY BE FAR AWAY," Ghostwriter wrote, "BUT THIS IS STILL TEAMWORK."

"YOU'RE RIGHT," Lenni wrote. "I JUST WISH MY TEAMMATES WERE HERE."

"HEY, PITCHER!" Ghostwriter wrote. "LAY IT INTO MY GLOVE."

Lenni smiled. So what if he had the wrong sport? It was great to have a helping hand. "THANKS, GHOSTWRITER. LET'S GET STARTED."

It wasn't easy. Lenni had so many notes, she didn't know where to start. "I'LL JUST TELL MY STORY," she decided. " 'I WAS BORN TWELVE YEARS AGO HERE IN NEW YORK. . . .' "

"LENNI? IS THIS A NOVEL?"

"RIGHT. I GUESS I DON'T HAVE TO GO BACK THAT FAR. 'ONE DAY LAST WEEK I DRESSED REALLY COOL.' "

"COOL?"

"Forget it. It sounds wrong anyway." Lenni decided she had the wrong approach. This wasn't for her, it was for the whole school.

" 'KIDS LIKE WEARING COOL CLOTHES,' " she began. That was better. Now she went back over the notes she'd made when she talked to her friends. She crossed out all the ideas that seemed too personal, and put a star next to the things that seemed most important. Those were the points she'd definitely try to cover in her speech.

Then she leaned back in her chair and looked over the notes again. They were really a mess, but this time she had a feeling the rap wasn't going to be so hard to do. "READY FOR MY FAST BALL?" she wrote to Ghostwriter. Then she sharpened her pencil and got to work.

By the time she finished writing, it was just starting to get dark outside. Maybe they're still playing, she thought hopefully. As soon as detention was over, she gathered her things and raced down to the playground.

"Go, Hurston!" she yelled as she approached the basketball court. It didn't take her long, though, to figure out that things weren't going well for her team. Jamal had the ball, but within moments a boy from the other team intercepted it. He raced down the court and made a basket

before the Hurston team knew what was happening.

Uh oh, Lenni thought as she sat down on the sideline.

As she watched, the kids from Atlantic Avenue made three more baskets. Her friends were beginning to look like all their energy had been zapped.

And then time ran out. The kids from Atlantic Avenue started leaping around the court giving each other high-fives. Lenni's friends dragged themselves over to the stands.

"Good try, you guys," Lenni said to them.

They looked up at her like sad sheep. "Now they've won three in a row," Alex sighed.

"I'm sorry I wasn't here with you," Lenni said.

"You shouldn't be," Jamal told her.

"I still think Hurston's a cooler school," Gaby piped in at last.

"How's the rap, Lenni?" Tina asked.

"Done. Here, I'll do it for you." She dug into her bag and pulled out a sheet of paper with the words written on it. She read it to the kids and got them smiling for the first time in hours.

"I think it's perfect," Tina said.

"Maybe we should have all gone to study hall," Jamal said. "I can't wait to hear you perform tomorrow."

"That's funny," Lenni said. "I can."

SORTING IT ALL OUT

Do you ever start to write something and find out you have too much information? That's what happened to Lenni when she started her rap. The other kids gave her too many good ideas to fit into one song.

Here are some things to do when you've got more information than you can handle.

- Narrow down your topic. For example, if you started off writing about food, maybe now you'll just write about french fries.
- Choose a special angle so you don't have to include all the information you have. It would be tough, for example, to write everything there is to know about french fries. Focus instead on how they taste.
- Decide which information is the most important, and leave out the rest.

Now try writing a rap or poem about something you care a lot about, keeping these points in mind.

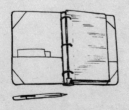

The next morning Lenni woke up with butterflies in her stomach. They got more and more active as the day went on.

"I think I'm going to freak out before seven o'clock," she told Alex and Jamal after school.

"Better not," Jamal said. "All the kids are getting warnings now. The whole school's going crazy about the dress code. We need you!"

"You're not making me feel any less nervous," Lenni said.

"Maybe we just need to get your mind off the meeting," Jamal said. "Want to go see a movie?"

"I have a better idea," Alex said. "Gaby and Tina have finished their video. Let's go check it out."

Lenni and Jamal agreed that it was a great idea. They headed over to Tina's.

"You're here to see our video!" Gaby exclaimed.

Tina rewound the tape to start, and the kids sat back to watch it.

"Hi. I'm investigative reporter Gaby Fernandez. We're

here at Zora Neale Hurston School to report on—the Dress Code!"

Lenni, Jamal, and Alex sat bolt upright. "You're what?"

"I thought your tape was going to be on what it's like to go to middle school," put in Jamal.

"In a way it is," explained Tina. "You'll see."

The video showed kids and teachers going in and out of the school. A few of the teachers wore jeans. Tina had done some good close-up shots of the jeans. Tina even got a shot of Ms. Willow wearing a blue dress—without a collar.

Gaby interviewed a bunch of kids. "I got in trouble for wearing a short skirt," complained one very tall girl. "But my friend Maria was wearing an even shorter skirt. Nobody noticed—maybe because she's short."

"The science teacher, Mr. Semberi, gave me a warning. He said a turtleneck shirt doesn't have a collar. But my mom bought it for me. *She* thinks it has a collar. And she's not happy that half my clothes are suddenly against the rules." That complaint came from an eighth-grade boy.

A young teacher stared into the camera. "Frankly, I'm all for a dress code," he said. "I remember what it was like when I was a kid, trying to keep up. It's easier, and fairer, if everybody dresses in neat, simple clothes."

"Bet he's related to Ms. Willow," Lenni muttered. But she had to admit he had some points when Gaby interviewed him some more.

"I know the kids are upset this week. The code is new. Everybody is trying to figure out what fits the code and what doesn't. And it doesn't help that somebody keeps tearing down Ms. Willow's dress code rules from the bulletin board."

The final scene in the video was a long-distance shot of five girls coming out of the school. They were all wearing long skirts, blouses with floppy collars, and boots. As the camera watched them come down the school steps, Gaby held up a handwritten sign in front of the camera: LENNI'S FAN CLUB, it said.

"The end!" Gaby said, obviously thrilled by Alex, Lenni, and Jamal's clapping.

"I've got a brainstorm," Alex said, excited. "If we can set it up, we'll show your video at the PTA meeting just before Lenni does her rap. It will be a double whammy!"

Tina was a bit shy about showing her video to a group of middle-school parents and teachers. "What if they think it's too childish—too . . ."

"Elementary?" laughed Jamal. "Don't worry—it's not."

Jamal and Alex decided to head back to school right away to persuade Mr. Brown to set up some TV screens in the auditorium. Lenni went home to change and meet her dad. He was taking her to the meeting. "Can't wait to hear you sing," he had said. Tina persuaded her mother to come. Jamal's grandmother arranged to meet Jamal at the PTA. The Fernandez family planned to bring Gaby along anyway, so everything was taken care of.

At the school Mr. Kent had arranged for Lenni and the other kids to sit with him in the auditorium. There was a lot of talking at the beginning that the kids found pretty boring, but finally Mr. Kent was called up onstage to introduce Lenni.

"Ladies and gentlemen," he said to the audience. "As some of you may know, Hurston Middle School has recently started a dress code. Many of the students are unhappy about the new rules, and they've asked if they might explain their concerns to you this evening. Please give your attention to Ms. Lenni Frazier. Lenni," he said, beckoning her toward the stage.

Lenni walked up the stairs to the stage and stood behind the podium. Mr. Kent tilted the microphone toward her mouth, then returned to his seat.

Lenni cleared her throat. Why was she so nervous? She could barely think straight, much less deliver her rap! She looked down at her paper.

All of a sudden the words scrambled up. "HAVE FUN, LENNI!" Ghostwriter wrote before he put the words back to normal. Lenni smiled and felt herself relax. Okay, she thought. Here I go.

"I'm not very good at writing speeches," she told the audience. Her voice was a little shaky at first, but she could feel it getting stronger. "So I've written a rap about the dress code instead. Some friends of mine, Gaby Fernandez and Tina Nguyen, made a videotape about the dress code that I'm going to show you first." She reached over to the VCR under the TV on the stage and put the tape in. She hit the start button. While the video played, Lenni got a chance to check out the audience. In the back were a couple of girls who were wearing long "Lenni outfits." Some of

them were with their mothers. The mothers were wearing
long skirts and boots, too. She looked for her dad. He was
in the middle, talking head to head with a woman in a navy
blue dress. Lenni's dad was talking very seriously to the
woman. She was smiling. At one point they glanced up at
the stage. Lenni was horrified. Her dad was talking to Ms.
Willow. Ms. Willow of the fangs and horns! Ms. Willow
of the dress code!

As Lenni began her rap, a quiet ripple of laughter broke
out in the audience. Lenni was afraid they weren't taking
her seriously, but when she looked up, all she saw were
smiling, approving faces. Her father winked at her.

"Kids wear blue jeans,
Miniskirts, and leggings.
Kids wear high tops, baggy pants, and earrings.
Kids wear clothes with kid appeal,
Clothes that show just how we feel.

"Now a dress code
(Really more a stress code)
Means that we can't dress up in our best mode.
Can't be funky, can't be cool,
Can't be us when we're in school.

"Why can't we choose
Worn-out shirts and tennis shoes?
Why does neon get such bad reviews?
Just what's wrong with jewelry, denim?
And why do teachers get to wear 'em?

"We like changing,
We like rearranging,
We like to be different—that's the main thing.
Why can't clothes reflect the day?
The mood we're in? The sports we play?

"I know you teach
Respect for free speech.
'Speak out! Write down! Express yourself!'
 you all preach.
Please let Hurston kids express
Our moods, ourselves, in how we dress."

As soon as Lenni finished the last line, her dad, Mr. Kent, and her friends jumped up to their feet and started clapping wildly. So did Alex and Jamal's families. But that wasn't all. The other parents and teachers in the audience were also clapping for Lenni, and a few of them even stood up, too.

By the end of the meeting Lenni and all of the kids were pretty happy. Not that the PTA just decided to get rid of the dress code. A lot of parents and teachers seemed to support it. But after hearing all sides—many times (Gaby said she had no idea grown-ups could talk so much)—the PTA decided to take a hard look at the dress code. A mother who was a lawyer pointed out that some kinds of dress codes might even be against the law. Ms. Willow said she just wanted to make life simpler and more organized for the kids at Hurston. So a committee

of parents, teachers, school officials, and one kid—Lenni—was formed.

"But I still don't think we should have a dress code at all," Lenni whispered to Jamal when they made the announcement.

Jamal whispered back, "You have a vote on the committee. If you think a dress code is bad, you can vote against it! That's your right."

On the way out of the meeting Lenni and her friends ran into Ms. Willow.

"That was an interesting presentation, Lenni," Ms. Willow said to her. "A very nice rap, too. I liked your images. They were very sharp."

Lenni shot a nervous look at Alex and Jamal.

"You know, the dress code you and your friends found was a very old one. I was so surprised to see your questions attached to it that I didn't know what to say to all of you. I can't imagine where you found it. It's so ridiculous. Imagine—no sneakers! No blue jeans for boys!"

"You mean that's not the one you were following?" Lenni asked.

"No," Ms. Willow said. "It's very outdated. Where did you find it?"

Lenni suddenly felt like she'd made a huge mistake. "I guess we jumped to the wrong conclusions," she apologized.

"Well, maybe you're not the only one who jumped to conclusions, then, Lenni," Ms. Willow said with a slight sigh. "You know, I didn't realize why you cared so much about the dress code. I thought you were just trying to make life hard for a substitute principal."

Lenni breathed a sigh of relief and smiled at Alex and Jamal.

"So, Lenni, why don't you come to my office tomorrow and we'll discuss your ideas. We might as well get a head start on the committee meetings."

"You mean you don't mind that I'm on the dress code committee?"

"Mind?" Ms. Willow said with a laugh. "It was my idea!"

When Ms. Willow was gone, Lenni turned to Alex and Jamal. "Can you believe it? I thought she'd hate me forever."

Just then Gaby and Tina came running up. Gaby was so excited, she couldn't talk. "That's a first," her brother whispered to Jamal. Then he gave Gaby a quick hug. Nothing too much, just enough to let her know she did a good job. "What teamwork!" Alex said. "Now if only we could learn to have it on the basketball court . . ."

"Next year, Alex," Jamal said with a laugh. "Next year."

That night Lenni and her dad celebrated the success of the meeting with a big meal of take-out Chinese food.

"Still feel like switching schools?" Lenni's dad asked her when they sat down at the kitchen table.

"Nah," she said, loading her chopsticks with sesame noodles. "I've got an important job to do at Hurston now."

"By the way," Max said, "I meant to tell you. Ms.

Willow is actually a pretty nice woman. She likes jazz. I recognized her tonight. Sometimes she comes to one of the clubs where I play."

Max smiled and munched thoughtfully on an egg roll. Lenni watched him for a few minutes. He didn't seem quite his usual self . . . sort of more quiet than usual.

"How's everything going, Dad?" she asked him.

"Oh, okay," he said mildly.

"You sure?"

"Well, I've got a few things on my mind. But nothing you need to worry about. Come on, this is supposed to be a celebration!"

"Dad," Lenni said, putting down her chopsticks and crossing her arms across her chest. "Come on. I know it's nice to think you can do things on your own. But sometimes it's important to ask for help, you know?"

Her father smiled at her and sighed. "Well, I guess I should tell you. I've been given a new project to work on."

"A piece to compose?" Lenni asked excitedly. "That's great!"

"In a way."

"Dad, you love to write jazz!" Lenni exclaimed.

"I know," he said. "But that's the problem. This isn't jazz. You're never going to believe this, Lenni. In fact, I can hardly believe it myself, but this group has asked me to write a rap for them!"

"A rap! No way! That's totally awesome!" Lenni was grinning from ear to ear. Her dad didn't look as excited, though. Then he took out a sheet of paper. He'd written his first attempt on it.

Lenni understood why her dad wasn't so happy about his rap. It was pretty lame. "I guess rap's not really your thing, is it, Dad?"

He shook his head. "It's too—I don't know. Too young for me."

One look and Lenni wrote a couple of changes on her dad's rap. Then she noticed something happening on the refrigerator behind her dad's head. Ghostwriter was rearranging the magnetic letters that were stuck on it. Lenni read the message and nodded—she'd had just the same thought. "Listen, Dad," she said with a smile. "I bet I know where I can get you some help."

"Oh yeah?" her father asked, brightening up.

Lenni nodded confidently. "There's this group around here. They're very cool, trust me. I think they know a thing or two about writing raps. What do you say I round 'em up for you?"

Max smiled knowingly. "I think that would be just great," he said happily.

"Here! Want a fortune cookie?" Lenni asked, tossing one over to her dad. "What does your fortune say?"

"Hmmm. 'You know where to find best help,'" Max read. He looked up at Lenni and smiled. "I already knew that!"

Lenni broke open her cookie and read her fortune out loud: "'Tips grow rare.' Now what's that supposed to mean?"

"Must be a hint from some restaurant owner trying to make an extra buck," Max said.

"That's no fortune," Lenni said with disappointment.

She looked down at the fortune again, but this time a huge smile broke out on her face. Ghostwriter had scrambled the letters to make a new message: "GO RAP WRITERS!!!!"

Lenni laughed and tucked the fortune inside her pocket. This one was for her and all her friends.

ATTENTION ALL WRITERS!

Or should I say "Yo, rappers"?
I guess my dad's been taking a nap.
Sure, jazz has pizzazz, but writing rap is a snap!
I know how, but you can show him now.
You can write about bowling or boxing, hiking or biking,
    beekeeping or sightseeing or juggling without struggling.
Just don't forget rhyming and timing and onomatopoeia.
Now you're on your own, so good luck—I'll see ya!

                      —Lenni

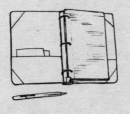

PRESENTING...
two magazines from the people who bring you GHOSTWRITER...

KID CITY MAGAZINE
Makes reading, language skills and learning fun. Educates and entertains through stories, puzzles, word games, projects and features. Perfect for Sesame Street Graduates! Ten issues for just $14.97.

3-2-1 CONTACT MAGAZINE
Award winning articles about Nature, Science and Technology. Each issue is packed with puzzles, projects, and challenging Square One TV math pages ...All designed to help your child learn while having fun. Ten issues for just $16.97.

To order the magazine of your choice, send payment to:

Your Magazine Choice
P.O. Box 52000
Boulder, Colorado 80322

(Please allow 5 to 6 weeks for delivery.)

DA53 11/92

Ghost writer™

MORE FUN-FILLED GHOSTWRITER BOOKS

☒ **A MATCH OF WILLS**   29934-4
by Eric Weiner $2.99/$3.50 in Canada

☐ **THE GHOSTWRITER DETECTIVE GUIDE:**   48069-3
Tools and Tricks of the Trade
by Susan Lurie $2.99/$3.50 in Canada

☐ **COURTING DANGER AND OTHER STORIES**   48070-7
by Dina Anastasio $2.99/$3.50 in Canada

☐ **DRESS CODE MESS**   48071-5
by Sara St. Antoine $2.99/$3.50 in Canada

☐ **THE BIG BOOK OF KIDS' PUZZLES**   37074-X
by P.C. Russell Ginns $1.25/$1.50 in Canada

☐ **THE MINI BOOK OF KIDS' PUZZLES**   37073-1
by Denise Lewis Patrick $.99/$1.25 in Canada

Bantam Books, Dept DA55, 2451 South Wolf Road, Des Plaines, IL
60018
Please send me the items I have checked above. I am enclosing $
_____ (please add $2.50 to cover postage and handling). Send check
or money order, no cash or C.O.D's please.

Mr/Mrs_____

Address _____

City/State_____ Zip_____
Please allow four to six weeks for delivery.
Prices and availability subject to change without notice.   DA55 11/92